SCIENCE
QUESTIONS & ANSWERS

Outdoor Science

Anita Ganeri

Dillon Press
New York

First American publication 1993 by Dillon Press, Macmillan Publishing Company,
866 Third Avenue, New York, NY 10022

Macmillan Publishing Company is part of the Maxwell Communication Group of Companies.

First published by Evans Brothers Limited,
2A Portman Mansions, Chiltern Street, London W1M 1LE

Printed in Hong Kong

10   9   8   7   6   5   4   3   2   1

Library of Congress Cataloging-in-Publication Data
Ganeri, Anita, 1961-
    Outdoor science / Anita Ganeri.
        p. cm.—(Science questions & answers)
    Includes index.
    Summary: Answers such questions as "Why is night dark?"
"Where does space begin?" and "What is lightning?"
    ISBN 0–87518–579–7
    1. Sun—Miscellanea—Juvenile literature. 2. Astonomy—Miscellanea—Juvenile literature.
3. Meteorology—Miscellanea—Juvenile literature. [1. Sun—Miscellanea. 2. Astronomy—Miscellanea.
3. Meteorology—Miscellanea. 4. Questions and answers.] I. Title. II. Series.
QB521.5.G35 1993
500—dc20   93-13125

Acknowledgments

The author and publishers would like to thank the following
for her valuable help and advice:
Sally Morgan MA, MSc, MIBiol

Illustrations: Virginia Gray - pages 6, 9, 13, 18, 20, 22, 24, 26, 28, 32, 33, 34, 37, 39
Maps: Jillian Luff of Bitmap Graphics - pages 14, 16, 25, 26, 29, 42, 44
Editors: Catherine Chambers and Jean Coppendale
Design: Monica Chia
Production: Peter Thompson

For permission to reproduce copyright material the author
and publishers gratefully acknowledge the following:
Cover photographs: (main picture) Storm over Tuscon, Arizona, USA, Warren Faidley, Oxford Scientific Films, (bottom left)
Winter sunset, London, Robert Francis, The Hutchison Library, (top right) A 'wind farm', California, USA, Alex Bartel,
Skogarfoss, Southern Iceland, Robert Francis, The Hutchison Library.
Page 7 - (top left) Frank Lane Picture Agency, (bottom left) Robert Harding Picture Library; page 8 - (left) Eric Crichton, Bruce Coleman
Limited, (right) Anthony King; page 10 - (top) Robert Carr, Bruce Coleman Limited, (bottom) Tony Craddock, Science Photo Library;
page 11 - (top left) John Cancalosi, Bruce Coleman Limited, (bottom left) Mark Boulton, Bruce Coleman Limited, (right) William
Smithey Jr, Planet Earth Pictures; page 12 - (left) Anthony King, (right) Sally Morgan, Ecoscene; page 13 - (top left) N. A. Callow, Robert
Harding Picture Library, (bottom left) Anthony King; page 15 - (top) Anna Zuckerman, Bruce Coleman Limited, (bottom) Anthony
King; page 17 - Zefa; page 18 - Andra Pradesh, The Hutchison Library; page 19 - (left) Colin Molyneux, The Image Bank, (right) Norman
Tomalin, Bruce Coleman Limited; page 20 - Anthony King; page 21 - (bottom left) Stan Osolinski, Oxford Scientific Films, (main
picture) Ronald Toms, Oxford Scientific Films, (top right) Stan Osolinski, Oxford Scientific Films; page 22 - Alvis Upitis, The Image
Bank; page 23 - (left) David Parker, Science Photo Library, (right) C. Newton, Frank Lane Picture Agency; page 24 - (left) Claude
Nuridsany and Marie Perennou, Science Photo Library, (right) Norman Tomalin, Bruce Coleman Limited; page 26 - Zefa; page 27 -
(left) Robert Harding Picture Library, (right) John Wells, Science Photo Library; page 28 - Anthony King; page 29 - Mary Clay, Planet
Earth Pictures; page 30 - (top) Zefa, (middle and bottom) Sally Morgan, Ecoscene; page 31 - (left) John Mead, Science Photo Library,
(main picture) Alex Bartel, Science Photo Library; page 32 - Robert Harding Picture Library; page 33 - Eric and David Hoskins, Frank
Lane Picture Agency; page 34 - (bottom left) G. M. Wilkins, Robert Harding Picture Library, (top right) Steven Kaufman, Bruce Coleman
Limited; page 35 - (left) Zefa, (top right) M. P. L. Fogden, Bruce Coleman Limited, (bottom right) John Topham, Bruce Coleman Limited;
page 36 - Jules Cowan, Bruce Coleman Limited; page 37 - Sally Morgan, Ecoscene; page 38 - (top) K. E. Deckart, Zefa, (bottom) Sally
Morgan, Ecoscene; page 39 - (top left) Christer Fredriksson, Bruce Coleman Limited, (bottom right) Robert Harding Picture Library;
page 40 - NASA, Science Photo Library; page 41 - (left) Royal Observatory, Edinburgh, Science Photo Library, (top and bottom right)
Anthony King; page 42 - (left) John Sanford, Science Photo Library; page 43 - (left) Ronald Royer, Science Photo Library, (right) M.
Newman, Frank Lane Picture Agency; page 44 - Anthony King; page 45 - (top left) NASA, Bruce Coleman Limited, (bottom right) NASA,
Science Photo Library.

Contents

Why do we need the sun? 6
- How hot is the sun?
- How does the sun's heat reach us?

How does a greenhouse help plants to grow? 8
- What is the greenhouse effect?

How can we use the sun's energy? 10
- How do we collect the sun's energy?

How do shadows form? 12
- Why are some shadows pale?
- Why do shadows change length?

Why is night dark? 14

Why do we have summer and winter? 16
- What is a leap year?

Why do puddles dry up in the sun? 18
- Why do we hang wet clothes out to dry?
- Why can we see our breath on a cold day?

What are clouds? 20
- How many types of clouds are there?

What makes it rain? 22
- What are rainbows?
- Why is the sky blue?
- Why is space black?

How do snowflakes form? 24
- Why does it hail?
- Why do we put salt on icy roads?
- How do solids, liquids and gases differ from each other?

What is air made of? 26
- What is the atmosphere?
- What is the ozone layer?

What is air pressure? 28
- How does the wind blow?
- What is windchill?
- What is a wind farm?

What is lightning? 32
- Why does thunder boom?

Why does smoke rise upward? 34
- What is a heat haze?

Why do leaves fall downward? 36
- Why do plant roots grow downward?
- Why does rain fall faster than snow?
- How do parachutes work?

Where does space begin? 40
- How big is the universe?

How far away are the stars? 42
- How many stars are there in space?
- Why do stars shine at night?

Why does the moon seem to change shape? 44
- What is the dark side of the moon?
- What are the dark patches on the moon?

Glossary 46
Further reading 46
Index 47

The words in **bold** in the text are explained in the Glossary on page 46.

Why do we need the sun?

The sun is just one of millions of stars in our **galaxy**, the Milky Way. It is just under 93 million miles away from the earth — a very long way indeed. But even at this distance, the sun is vitally important to all of us. Without the sun's heat and light, nothing could live or grow on earth. The earth would be too cold for anything to survive. There would be no light for plants to make their own food, so there would be nothing for us to eat.

How hot is the sun?

The sun is incredibly hot. Its surface temperature is 10,000 °F. At the sun's core, or center, the temperature reaches an amazing 27 million °F. This is where the sun's heat and light are made. Like other stars, the sun is made up mainly of hydrogen gas. It is so hot in the center of the sun that atoms (tiny particles) of hydrogen bump into each other and form another gas, called helium. As

The different layers and areas of the sun

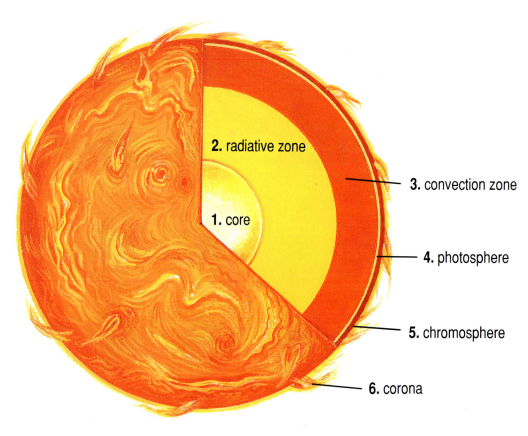

2. radiative zone

3. convection zone

1. core

4. photosphere

5. chromosphere

6. corona

1. energy made here
2. radiation of energy from core
3. energy carried away from core

4. visible layer of sun
5. rosy ring of gases around sun
6. outermost envelope of gases

this happens, huge amounts of heat and light energy are given off. The sun burns up about 700 million tons of hydrogen every second during these **reactions**. Luckily for us, the sun has enough hydrogen left to keep shining for at least another five billion years.

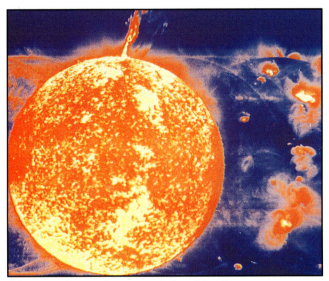
The sun is made up mainly of hydrogen.

Deserts are baked dry by the sun.

How does the sun's heat reach us?

The sun's heat travels through space and takes about 8.5 minutes to reach the earth. Heat travels in several different ways — by convection, conduction, and radiation, depending on what it has to travel through.

Heat from the sun travels to earth by radiation. This means that it travels in invisible rays, just like the rays of heat coming from a fire. This is the only way that heat can travel through space. Convection is how heat travels through liquids or gases, such as the sea and the air. Conduction is the way heat travels through solids. Space has no air. It is also empty, so heat cannot travel by either of these methods.

Less than a millionth of the heat that leaves the sun reaches the earth. Some heat is lost on its way through space and some will be **reflected** back into space. The rest is **absorbed** by the earth's atmosphere. There is no **atmosphere** around the moon, so it feels much hotter there.

 Did you know?

A piece of the sun's surface about the size of your thumbnail shines as brightly as at least 200,000 candles.

 Did you know?

The sun is about 868,000 miles wide. It is big enough to swallow up 1.3 million earths.

How does a greenhouse help plants to grow?

Plants use sunlight to help them make their food. They do this using a process called photosynthesis. Many plants also need warmth in order to grow, particularly if they come originally from warm countries. Gardeners often grow plants like these in greenhouses, where they are kept warm and are protected from the frost and wind.

The glass in the greenhouse is transparent, so sunlight can pass through it to the inside. The sunlight heats up all the objects in the greenhouse, including the plants. In turn, these objects give off heat. But the heat is not in the right form to pass back out through the glass. The glass traps the heat that builds up inside the greenhouse, heating up the air and keeping the plants warm.

! See for yourself

Try to make your own mini-greenhouses and grow some plants in them. Make some drainage holes in plant pots or yogurt containers and put a layer of stones at the bottom of them. Fill the pots with soil or **potting compost**. Plant some chick-peas or unroasted peanuts in the soil and water them well. The drainage holes and stones will keep the soil from getting waterlogged so the plants' roots will not rot. Cover the pots with plastic bags, held in place with rubber bands.

It should not be long before the first shoots appear. When the first leaves start to unfold, take the plants out of their "greenhouses" and stand them in a sunny place. If the plants stay in the greenhouses too long, the shoots will grow too tall as the plants try to search for the light.

Tropical palm trees thrive in a greenhouse.

Left: The "greenhouse" is made.
Right: The peanuts burst into leaves.

What is the greenhouse effect?

The earth's atmosphere works in a similar way to the greenhouse (see opposite page). It traps some of the sun's heat and stops it from escaping into space. This is called the greenhouse effect. It keeps the earth warm enough for plants and animals to survive.

But scientists are worried that too much heat is being trapped and that the earth may be getting too warm. Carbon dioxide is just one of the gases that help to trap heat. For millions of years, the amount of carbon dioxide in the atmosphere has been kept at just the right level to keep the earth at the correct temperature.

But people are upsetting the balance. They are increasing the amount of carbon dioxide in the atmosphere by

(see opposite page)

 Did you know?

Each year, an extra 400,000 million tons of carbon dioxide are being put into the air by cars and factories.

burning coal and oil, by burning down forests, and by creating air pollution in other ways. The extra gas released into the atmosphere may trap so much extra heat that the earth's temperature could rise by 4 to 7 °F by the year 2030. If it rises any higher than that, the ice at the poles could melt and drown many towns and cities along some coasts.

 Did you know?

A car **emits** four times its own weight in carbon dioxide every year.

atmosphere with normal amount of greenhouse gases

Pollution-free earth

atmosphere with concentrated greenhouse gases

The greenhouse effect

How can we use the sun's energy?

Each day, the earth receives enormous amounts of energy from the sun. This reaches us in the form of heat and light. We need this heat and light in order to survive (see pages 6 and 9). But scientists are now looking at other ways of using all this energy.

Everything we do or use needs energy to make it work. We get our energy from food. Cars get energy from gasoline. Televisions, refrigerators, kettles, and computers get their energy from the electricity supplied to them.

Most of this electricity comes from oil, gas, and coal, which are burned in huge power stations. But stocks of these fuels are running out. They also produce gases such as sulfur dioxide, which pollutes the air and causes problems such as acid rain. If we could turn some of the sun's energy into electricity, we would have a power supply that is not only cleaner but that would never run out. How do we go about doing this?

The white haze hanging over the town is polluted air.

 Did you know?

Scientists have worked out that the amount of solar energy reaching the earth each year is 15,000 times the amount of energy people on earth use each year.

The Odeillo solar power station in the Pyrenees Mountains, France

How do we collect the sun's energy?

The sun's energy is called solar energy. There are two ways of using it. In many hot countries, such as Greece and Israel, people have water-filled panels on the roofs of their houses. During the day, the sun heats up the water and it is piped around the house. It can be used for baths, showers, and washing the dishes.

Another way of collecting the sun's energy is with solar cells. They turn solar energy straight into electricity. Most solar cells are made of a substance called silicon. They used to be very expensive, but you can now buy them quite easily. You might already have some if you own a solar-powered calculator or watch. These have solar cells inside them.

Right: A close-up of some solar cells

Below: This solar panel in Kenya supplies hot water for washing.

How do shadows form?

Light travels in rays that go in straight lines. The light rays cannot bend to go around objects. They can only pass straight through objects that are transparent, like glass. Objects that only allow a little light to pass through are called translucent. Most objects are opaque. This means that light cannot pass through them at all. When light shines on an opaque object, a shadow forms on the other side of the object where light cannot reach. Your body is opaque, too. When the sunlight shines on you, you cast a shadow.

Why are some shadows pale?

The darkest shadow forms when light shines straight onto an object from a single point. The type of shadow formed behind the object is called umbra. If light hits the object at an angle, or from more than one point, a paler shadow forms a rim around the dark umbra. This lighter shadow is known as penumbra.

 See for yourself

To see how shadows form, make your own shadow pictures. Shine a flashlight at a wall. Put your hand out near the wall, so that the beam shines on your hand. Make a rabbit shadow or a bird.

A bird shadow has formed.

See for yourself

To make umbra and penumbra, hold your hand underneath a flashlight beam. You should see a very dark shadow, or umbra, in the middle. Around the edge there should be a lighter area of shadow, the penumbra.

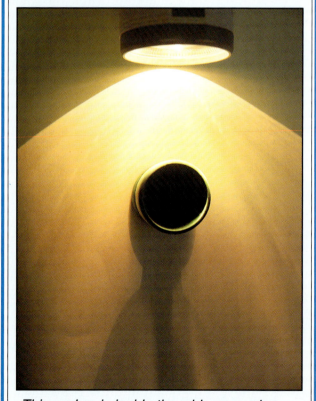

Thin umbra is inside the wide penumbra.

Why do shadows change length?

The size and shape of a shadow change with the size and position of the source of light. The length of the shadow you cast on the ground changes throughout the day. This is because the sun is higher or lower in the sky at different times of the day. Your shadow is longer in the morning or evening, when the sun is low in the sky. It is shorter at midday, when the sun is high in the sky.

Long shadows form in the morning and evening.

Midday shadows are short.

! See for yourself

You can use shadows to tell the time. As the sun seems to change position during the day, the shadow it casts moves as well. On a sundial, the shadows point to hour markings. You can make your own simple sundial using a stick and white cardboard.

On a sunny day, lay the cardboard on the ground and push the stick through the middle of it. Weight the corners of the cardboard down to keep it flat. Mark the position of the shadow on the cardboard every hour. Start early in the morning for the best results. On the next sunny day, replace your sundial in the same position and you will be able to tell the time.

? Did you know

Sometimes the moon is blocked out by the earth's shadow. This is called a lunar eclipse. It happens when the earth lies between the moon and the sun in a straight line.

Why is night dark?

The sun cannot reach all parts of our earth at the same time. This is why we are sometimes in darkness and at other times in light. The earth and the other planets in our solar system orbit, or travel around, the sun. As the earth travels around the sun, it also spins on its axis. This is an imaginary line running down the middle of the earth from the North Pole to the South Pole. The earth takes one year to orbit the sun once, and it takes 24 hours to spin around once on its axis.

The sun shines on the side of the earth facing it. Places on this side have daylight. No light reaches the other side, so places there are dark. As the earth spins on its axis, the place where you live moves from light into darkness once every 24 hours. This gives you day and night.

 Did you know?

A day on earth is 24 hours long. But a day on Venus lasts for 243 earth days. This is the time it takes Venus to spin around once on its axis. On Jupiter, though, a day is just 9.9 earth hours long.

 Did you know?

You cannot feel the earth spinning on its axis because everything on the earth, including you, is moving at the same speed.

As the earth spins on its axis, different places face the sun at different times. This gives us day and night.

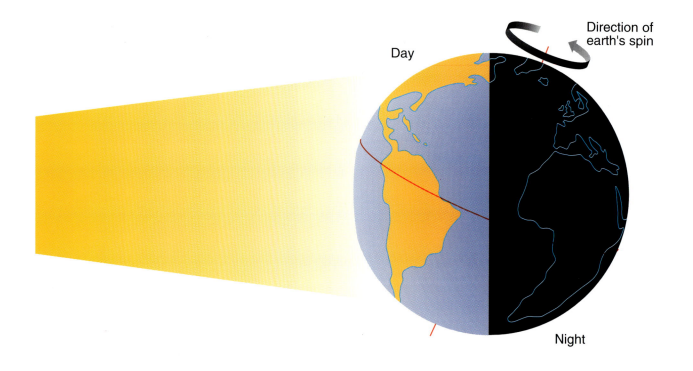

Day

Direction of earth's spin

Night

Did you know?

The North Pole is light for 24 hours a day in June and July. This is known as the "Land of the Midnight sun." At the same time of year, the South Pole is in darkness for 24 hours each day. In December and January, everything changes: The South Pole has continuous daylight and the North Pole has continuous night.

Midnight in Antarctica and it's still light.

 See for yourself

Try this simple experiment to see how the earth's spin gives us day and night. You will need a flashlight for the sun. Use an apple or orange for the earth and skewer it carefully with a stick or knitting needle so that you can hold it and move it around easily. Mark the **equator** around the center of the earth. Hold up the stick and turn the earth counterclockwise, tilting it on its axis. Ask a friend to shine the light on the fruit. You will see how different parts of the earth move into the light to give day, then out of the light to give night.

 Did you know?

The earth spins in a counter clockwise direction. As the earth spins, the sun seems to move across the sky, rising in the east and setting in the west. In fact, the sun does not move at all.

 Did you know?

In the **northern hemisphere**, summer begins on June 21. This is the longest day of the year. Winter begins on December 21. This is the shortest day of the year.

Why do we have summer and winter?

The seasons change as different parts of the earth lean toward or away from the sun. The earth is tilted on its axis, which means that it leans slightly to one side, at an angle. As the earth travels around the sun, its tilt makes the poles take turns in leaning toward the sun and getting more heat and light. This is what causes the seasons.

When the North Pole leans toward the sun, the northern hemisphere gets closer to the sun and has summer. The days are warm and sunny.

Meanwhile, the **southern hemisphere** leans away from the sun and has winter. The days are gloomy and cold. When the South Pole leans toward the sun, the northern hemisphere has winter and the southern hemisphere has summer. In between winter and summer, the hemispheres have spring or autumn.

Places near the equator do not have seasons, though. They are never tilted away from the sun, so they are always very hot.

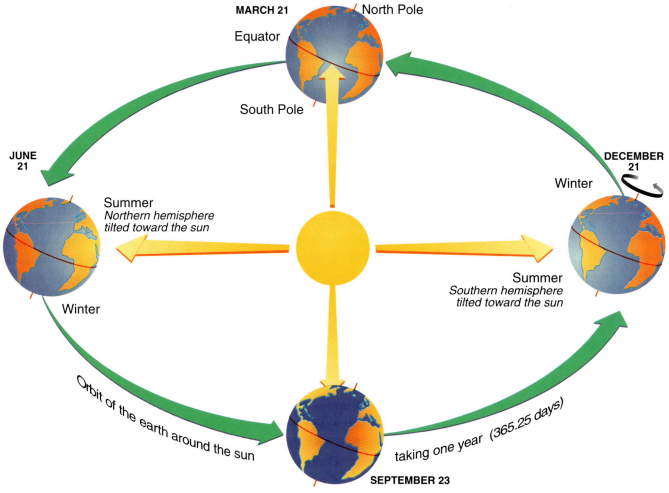

The seasons change as the earth moves around the sun.

What is a leap year?

A year is the length of time it takes for the earth to travel once around the sun. There are usually 365 days in a year, divided into 12 months. But the earth does not travel around the sun in exactly 365 days. It takes a bit longer than that — about 365.25 days. So an extra day is added to February (as the 29th) every four years. This 366-day year is called a leap year and uses up the four extra quarter days. You can tell if a year is a leap year if it divides exactly by four. So, for example, 1990 was not a leap year because 1990 does not divide exactly by four. Can you work out when the next leap year will be?

 Did you know?

A year on Pluto lasts for 164.8 earth years. This is how long Pluto takes to travel around the sun.

 Did you know?

An earth year is really 365.24219878 days long. To make calculations easier, we round it off to 365.25 days.

Above: A sunny summer's day

Right: A snowy day in winter in the same place

Why do puddles dry up in the sun?

In warm weather, any puddles left by a rain shower quickly dry up in the sun and disappear. But where does the rainwater go when it disappears? The answer is that it evaporates. This means that the sun's heat makes the liquid water turn into its invisible gas form, which is called water vapor. The **molecules** of water vapor then escape into the air and spread out.

Evaporation actually takes place all the time. The water molecules are constantly passing into the air. The puddle would eventually dry up of its own accord as long as there were no more showers. But on a warm day, the sun heats the water and causes it to evaporate more quickly than it would otherwise.

There is always some water vapor in the air. It plays a very important part

⚠ See for yourself

You can use a simple experiment to see how water evaporates in the sun. Place a small saucer of water on a sunny windowsill. How long does it take to dry up and disappear? Try the same experiment using a dark-colored and a light-colored saucer. The water in the dark saucer will heat up and evaporate more quickly than the water in the other saucer. The darker color absorbs more heat than the lighter color, which bounces a lot of the heat back into the air. This keeps the light-colored saucer, and its water, cooler.

in the weather (see page 20). But warm air can hold more water vapor than cold air. This is why the water from the puddles passes easily into the air on a warm day.

The bed of a dried-up river in India

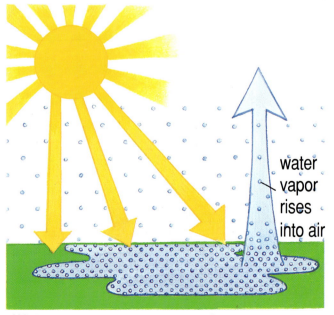

water vapor rises into air

Water evaporates on a sunny day.

Why do we hang wet clothes out to dry?

The best time to hang wet clothes out to dry is on a sunny, windy day. The sun dries the clothes by evaporation, just as it dries up the puddle. The sun's heat turns the droplets of water in the wet clothes into invisible water vapor, which vanishes into the air.

As the water molecules pass from the clothes into the air, they create a layer of "wet" air around the clothes. If the air is very wet, the clothes will take a long time to dry. This is because the air is already **saturated** with water vapor, so it cannot absorb any more moisture from the wet clothes. The clothes will dry more quickly if the wind is blowing. This is because the wind carries the wet air away and replaces it with drier air, which can absorb moisture.

Wet clothes dry by evaporation.

⚠ See for yourself

To see condensation at work, breathe out onto a cold surface such as a mirror or windowpane. Your breath will cloud over the glass. After a while, you should be able to see tiny droplets of water trickling down the mirror or window.

Condensation on a window

Why can we see our breath on a cold day?

If water vapor cools down again, it turns back into liquid water (see page 20). This process is called condensation. When you breathe out on a cold day, does your breath make a white cloud? This is because of condensation. The air you breathe out contains some water vapor. When this comes into contact with the cold air, it cools down and turns into tiny droplets of water.

What are clouds?

Clouds are formed by condensation (see page 19). As the sun shines down on the earth, it heats the ground, rivers and oceans, and the air above them. This air **expands** as it gets warm and takes water vapor with it. This air is very light and rises upward. As it gets higher up in the sky, it cools down again. Then some of the water vapor it contains condenses and turns into tiny droplets of liquid water. It takes millions and millions of these droplets to form a cloud. Clouds also form when water vapor condenses on specks of smoke or dust in the air.

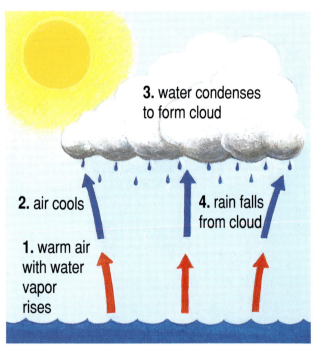

3. water condenses to form cloud

2. air cools

4. rain falls from cloud

1. warm air with water vapor rises

Clouds are made up of millions of water droplets.

 Did you know?

If a cloud moves into warmer air, it evaporates and vanishes. If it moves into even colder air, the water droplets may freeze and fall as snow.

 See for yourself

To make your own cloud, you will need a glass bottle, an ice cube, and some hot (but not boiling) water. Ask an adult to help you with this experiment. Fill the bottle with the hot water and let it stand for a few minutes. Then pour most of the water away. Leave about 2 inches in the bottom of the bottle. Balance the ice cube on top of the bottle. Then stand the bottle against a dark background and watch what happens. The hot water will heat the air above it. This air will rise up. When it hits the cold ice cube, the water vapor in the rising air should condense to form a small cloud.

You can see the water vapor moving around in the "cloud."

How many types of clouds are there?

Clouds come in two basic shapes. Puffy, cauliflowerlike clouds form when warm air rises quickly in huge bubbles. These are called cumulus clouds. Some clouds form in layers when air rises more slowly and spreads out in the sky. These are called stratus clouds.

There are ten main types of clouds. They form at different heights in the sky. High clouds form up to 8 miles above the ground. Medium clouds form up to 4 miles above the ground. Low clouds form up to 1 mile above the ground.

Right: Cirrocumulus "'mackerel" clouds

Below: Cumulus and altocumulus clouds

Inset: Wispy mare's tail cirrus clouds

What makes it rain?

Rain forms inside clouds, particularly inside clouds that are dark and gray. Sometimes, hundreds of the tiny droplets of water inside a cloud collide with one another to form larger drops. When these drops are big enough, they fall from the cloud as rain. It takes over a thousand droplets to make a raindrop. Rain also forms if snow melts on its way down to earth. Sleet is a mixture of rain and snow.

Raindrops are often thought to be shaped like teardrops. In fact, they look more like circles with the bottoms cut off. Raindrops are usually about as wide as the base of this letter "b".

A tropical downpour

 Did you know?

The wettest place in the world is Tutunendo in Colombia, South America. It has an average of 460 inches of rain a year. This is enough to cover six people standing on top of each other's shoulders.

 Did you know?

The water on the earth is used again and again. It moves around the world largely by evaporation and condensation (see pages 19 and 20). The sun's heat evaporates water from the land, rivers, and seas. It rises into the air as water vapor. As it rises, it condenses and forms clouds. Then rain or snow falls from the clouds, back onto the land and into the rivers and seas. No new water is ever made.

The water cycle happens all the time, reusing the earth's water supply.

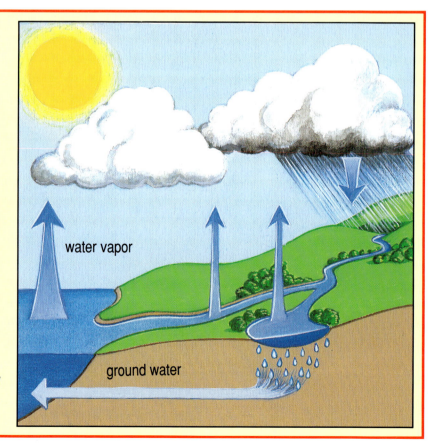

water vapor

ground water

What are rainbows?

The light coming from the sun is called white light. But it is made up of a mixture of different colors. The main colors in sunlight are red, orange, yellow, green, blue, indigo, and violet. These are known as the colors of the spectrum. They are the colors you see in a rainbow.

A prism splits white light into the colors of the spectrum.

If you shine white light through a triangular block of glass, it splits up into the colors of the spectrum. The block of glass is called a prism. As the light rays pass through the prism, they are bent, or refracted. Each color bends a slightly different amount. This makes the colors fan out so you can see each one quite clearly.

When the sun comes out during a shower of rain, the sunlight shines through the raindrops. They act like tiny prisms and split the sunlight up into its different colors. The colors form a rainbow in the sky. Red is always at the top and violet at the bottom. To see a rainbow, you must stand with your back to the sun.

Why is the sky blue?

Blue is one of the colors that make up white light. When the sun is high in the sky, light has only a short distance to travel to reach earth. But as it travels, it hits dust particles in the atmosphere. These particles scatter the light. Blue light scatters before any of the other colors in the spectrum, so it is the blue light that we can see. The other colors hit the earth before they are scattered. After sunrise and before sunset, most of the sunlight passes straight through the gas molecules. But they scatter the blue light all over the sky. This is why the sky looks blue.

But at dawn and dusk, when the sun is low, light has to travel farther, so other colors get scattered before they reach the earth. This is why we get beautiful red and orange sunsets.

At sunrise and sunset, the sky is often a dramatic orange-red color.

Why is space black?

Space has no air at all. It is a vacuum. So white light can pass straight through it without being scattered. The moon always has a black sky because it has no atmosphere to hold dust particles.

How do snowflakes form?

Snowflakes form inside clouds high up in the sky. These clouds are so cold that they contain ice crystals. More water freezes onto the crystals until, like raindrops, they are heavy enough to start falling to earth. As the crystals fall, they crash into other ice crystals inside the cloud and stick together to form snowflakes.

Snowflakes come in a range of shapes, from needle shapes to star shapes. But they all have six sides, and no two are ever the same. Next time it snows, look at some snowflakes, using a magnifying glass. How many different patterns can you find?

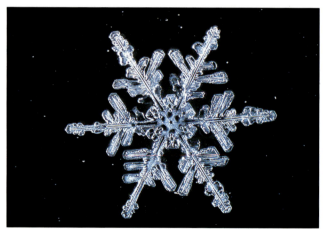

Snowflakes are all six-sided, but each is unique.

Why does it hail?

Hailstones are small balls of ice. Surprisingly, they do not often fall on cold winter days. They usually fall from thunderclouds on hot, sticky summer days. The air currents inside a thundercloud are so strong that they toss ice crystals up and down, and water freezes onto them in layers. When the crystals are about the size of peas, they fall as hailstones. Sometimes hailstones as big as tennis balls crash to the ground.

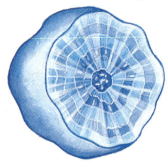

Left: Section through a hailstone

Below: A cluster of hailstones

Why do we put salt on icy roads?

In winter, sidewalks and roads may be covered with ice and snow. They can become very slippery and dangerous to walk on or drive along. In some places, people sprinkle salt on the roads to keep ice from forming.

When liquid water is cooled below a certain temperature, it turns into solid ice. This is called its freezing point. Water turns to ice at 32 °F. If the temperature does not rise above the freezing point in winter, the ice on the roads does not melt. But salty water has a lower freezing point than ordinary water. When people put salt on the winter roads, it mixes with the rain or snow to make salt water. The road will then take longer to ice over.

 Did you know?

When water is heated to 212 °F, it starts to boil. Different substances freeze and boil at different temperatures. Steel has to be heated to 2,550 °F before it melts. Mercury, a liquid metal that is used in thermometers, freezes at -38 °F.

 Did you know?

A molecule of water is made up of two atoms of hydrogen and one oxygen atom. The chemical symbol for water is H_2O.

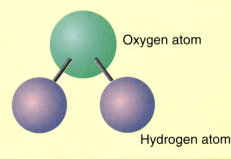

Oxygen atom

Hydrogen atom

How do solids, liquids, and gases differ from each other?

Most of the substances in the world appear in solid, liquid, or gas form. These are known as the three states of matter. Every substance is made up of tiny pieces, called molecules, that are made up of even tinier particles known as atoms. In solids, the molecules are packed closely together, held in place by **bonds**. This is why solids are rigid. In liquids, the bonds between the molecules break apart and are much looser. This is why liquids can flow. In gases, the molecules are even farther apart. This is why gases can spread out so easily.

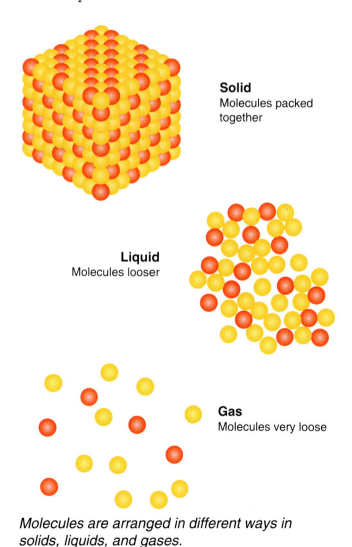

Solid
Molecules packed together

Liquid
Molecules looser

Gas
Molecules very loose

Molecules are arranged in different ways in solids, liquids, and gases.

What is air made of?

Hot-air balloons are filled with a light gas, helium, to make them rise into the air.

The air you breathe is made up of a mixture of different gases. About 78 percent of the air is nitrogen. Some 21 percent is oxygen. About 1 percent of the air is made up of the gas argon. There are also tiny amounts of carbon dioxide, helium, hydrogen, methane, neon, ozone, krypton, xenon, and water vapor in the air.

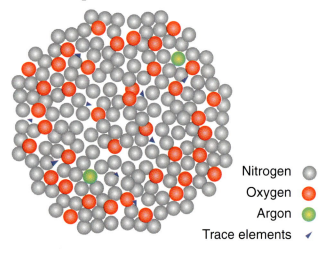

Nitrogen ⚪
Oxygen 🔴
Argon 🟢
Trace elements ◄

Air is made up of many different gases.

What is the atmosphere?

The atmosphere is a huge blanket of air that surrounds the earth. It is divided into different layers, as you can see in the diagram below. We live in the layer closest to the ground. This is called the troposphere. It reaches about 10 miles up into the sky. This is also where our weather is made. The highest layer is the exosphere, where satellites orbit the earth. It reaches a height of about 5,000 miles. Above it, there is space.

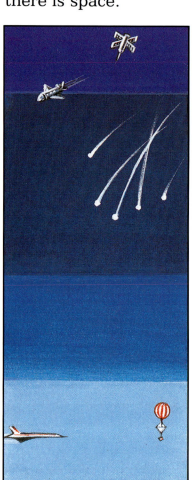

a satellite in the exosphere (300 to 5,000 miles)

a space shuttle crossing into the thermosphere (50 to 300 miles)

meteorites

the mesosphere (30 to 50 miles)

Concorde and a weather balloon in the stratosphere (7 to 30 miles)

passenger jet in the troposphere (0 to 7 miles)

The layers of the atmosphere

The atmosphere protects the earth from the burning effects of the sun's harmful ultraviolet rays. It also keeps the earth from getting too cold by preventing all of the earth's heat from escaping into space. The atmosphere is kept in place around the earth by the earth's gravity (see page 40). This keeps the atmosphere from floating off into space.

 Did you know?

Some 80 percent of the air in the atmosphere is found in the troposphere. There is less and less air the higher up you go. In space, there is no air at all.

Climbers run out of breath when they climb high up. Some even have to wear oxygen masks, although others try to climb to the tops of mountains without them.

What is the ozone layer?

A gas called ozone is found high up in the earth's atmosphere and low down on the ground. At ground level, the ozone is made mainly by gases from car exhaust fumes. These gases react in bright sunlight and change into ozone gas. This gas pollutes the air and can be poisonous to people and animals.

But high up, ozone occurs naturally and helps to protect life on earth. It forms a shield around the earth that keeps the sun's harmful ultraviolet rays from reaching us.

Since 1985, scientists have been worried that the amount of ozone gas in the layer is getting less and less. They have found patches of ozone that are so thin, they look like holes in the layer. These holes drift and split up all the time, but a very large one has been found over Antarctica. It is thought that man-made gases such as those in aerosol cans have thinned the ozone in this way.

Can you think what would happen if there was no ozone layer at all? The sun's harmful rays would reach the earth, causing skin cancers and eye cataracts, and damaging plants. To keep the ozone from disappearing, we have to stop releasing damaging gases into the air.

The white area shows the hole in the ozone layer over Antarctica in October 1991.

What is air pressure?

The air in the atmosphere presses down on the earth. This is called atmospheric pressure, or air pressure. The air also presses down on you, but you do not normally feel it.

Air pressure is different all over the world. It also changes from day to day, and this has a great effect on the weather. Cold air is heavy and sinks down toward the ground. This creates an area of high pressure. Warm air is light and rises upward. This creates an area of low pressure. Rising air pressure tends to bring settled, warm weather. Falling air pressure tends to bring wet, cloudy weather.

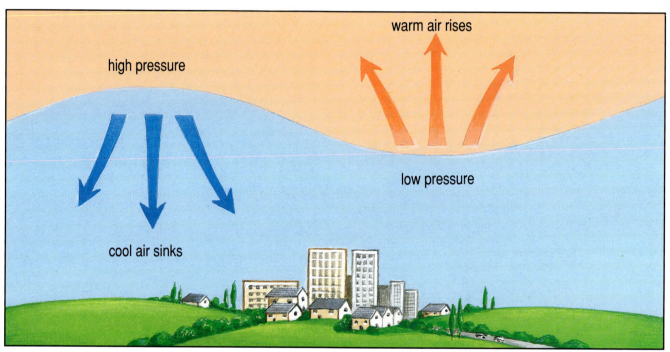

Areas of high and low pressure are created by air sinking or rising.

See for yourself

Try this simple experiment to see how heavy air is. Blow up two balloons. Make one a lot bigger than the other. Tie them to a stick or a coat hanger with string of the same length and the same distance from the center. Then hold or hang up the coat hanger. The bigger balloon should dip lower than the smaller one because the bigger balloon contains more air and is therefore heavier.

How does the wind blow?

Wind is air moving from place to place. You cannot see the wind itself, but you can feel it on your face and see its effect on trees or on smoke from chimneys. All over the world, cold air moves from areas of high pressure to areas of low pressure, where warm air has risen and made space for cold air to rush in. This is what makes the wind blow. But the wind does not blow in a straight line from the poles (areas of high pressure) to the equator (an area of low pressure). As the earth spins on its axis (see page 14), it makes the winds swing sideways. They swing to the right in the southern hemisphere and to the left in the northern hemisphere.

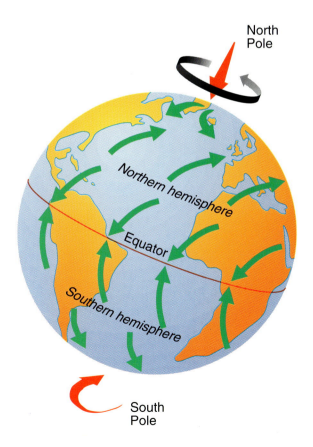

The winds are swung to the side as the earth spins on its axis. This is called the Coriolis effect.

 Did you know?

Winds are named according to the direction from which they blow. This means that a south wind is one that blows from the south. You can tell where the wind is coming from by holding a paper tissue up in the air and seeing which way it blows.

 Did you know?

The windiest place in the world is Commonwealth Bay in Antarctica. Here, gales blow at speeds of 200 miles an hour. But near the equator, there are areas of ocean where the wind does not blow for weeks on end.

Winds of 30 to 37 miles an hour can make trees sway, but winds of 43 to 50 miles an hour can break off small branches.

A windswept bristlecone pine in the Colorado Rockies. In some places, the wind blows very strongly, and mostly in one direction, all the time. This makes plants grow in the direction of the wind.

What is windchill?

If the wind is blowing strongly, it can feel much colder than it actually is. This is called the windchill factor. The wind draws heat away from your body, making you feel chilly. If the wind was blowing at 30 miles an hour and the temperature was -29 °F, you would freeze solid!

Different winds brings different types of weather. North winds bring cold weather, whereas south winds bring warmer weather.

A strong wind makes walking difficult.

 See for yourself

Meteorologists are scientists who study the weather. They measure wind direction and wind speed. You can make your own wind-speed-measuring device. You will need a protractor, some tape, a long piece of thread, and a table-tennis ball. Stick one end of the thread to the center of the protractor and the other end to the table-tennis ball. Hold the wind measure with the edge of the protractor toward the wind and see how far the wind blows the ball to each side. Read the angle that the thread reaches on the protractor. Then work out how fast the wind is blowing, using the table below.

ANGLE	MILES/HOUR
90°	0
80°	9
70°	12
60°	16
50°	19
40°	22
30°	27
20°	33

What is a wind farm?

Despite its name, you will not find any animals on a wind farm. A wind farm is a collection of machines called wind turbines. They look a bit like tall, thin windmills. They use the power of the wind to make electricity. The wind makes the turbine blades turn. This powers a generator, which produces electricity. Some of the biggest wind farms have been built in Denmark and in California. The wind farm at Altamont Pass, California, has more than 300 wind turbines.

 Did you know?

Hundreds of isolated villages in Mongolia get the electricity to power their television sets from wind turbines.

 See for yourself

Choose a cool, windy day and stand for two minutes facing the wind, holding a thermometer. Read the temperature on the thermometer and write it down. Now stand for two minutes in a sheltered spot away from the wind. Read the thermometer again. You should find that the temperature has risen. How many degrees warmer is it?

Main: Three-blade wind turbines in Altamont, California   **Inset**: A bow-shaped turbine

What is lightning?

Hot, sticky weather and towering, black cumulonimbus clouds are sure signs that a thunderstorm is on its way. Thunderstorms can be very dramatic, with flashes of lightning, booming thunder, gusty winds, and pouring rain. There may also be showers of hailstones (see page 24).

As a thundercloud grows, there is a lot of activity taking place inside it. Strong air currents bounce water droplets and pieces of ice up and down inside the cloud. These collide and rub together. The rubbing makes a force called an electrical charge.

The cloud is now charged with electricity. There are positive charges at the top of the cloud and negative charges at the bottom. The negative charges attract the positive charges and a giant spark of electricity jumps between them. You can see this spark as a flash of lightning. The lightning may also flash between the cloud and the ground.

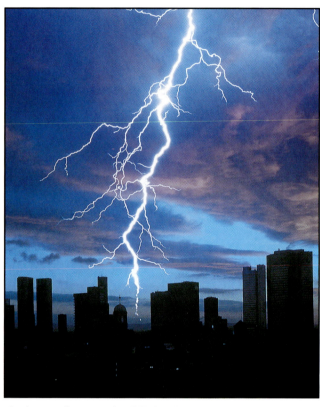

A dramatic streak of lightning

Lightning flashes within the cloud.

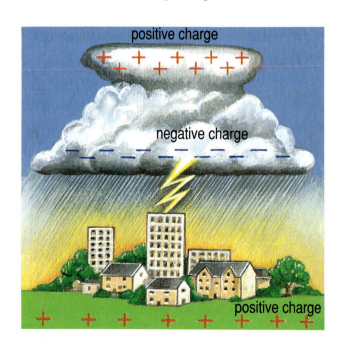

Lightning flashes to the ground.

See for yourself

Lightning is a type of electricity, called static electricity. It is the same type of electricity that makes your clothes crackle when you take them off. If you undress in the dark, you can even see sparks coming from your clothes. Sometimes static electricity can make your hair stand on end or crackle when you comb it. To see how strong static electricity is, comb your hair with a plastic comb. Then use the comb to pick up some small pieces of torn paper.

Why does thunder boom?

As the lightning streaks through the cloud, it heats the air around it to about 54,000 °F. The air gets so hot that it expands very quickly indeed. This is what causes the loud, booming noise of thunder. The thunder happens at exactly the same time as the lightning. But you see the lightning first. This is because light travels through the air faster than sound.

Did you know?

Thunderstorms are extremely powerful. If you could collect the energy from a single flash of lightning, it would be enough to light up a town for a year.

Did you know?

It is very dangerous to shelter under a tree during a thunderstorm. Lightning always takes the shortest path to the ground. It could hit the tree on its way.

A tree trunk burned by lightning

See for yourself

To find out how far away a thunderstorm is, count the number of seconds between the lightning and the thunder. Then divide the number of seconds by five. This will give the distance of the storm in miles.

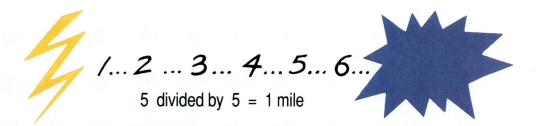

1... 2 ... 3... 4... 5... 6...

5 divided by 5 = 1 mile

Why does smoke rise upward?

A fire is one way of getting rid of old leaves and other garden waste. If there is no wind blowing, the smoke from the fire rises straight up into the air. This is because the heat from the fire is traveling through the air by convection (see page 7).

As the fire burns, it heats the air around it. This hot air rises because it is lighter than the colder air below. As it rises, it carries the heat and smoke from the fire upward with it. The colder air sinks downward to take the place of the warm air. This cold air is in turn heated by the fire and rises. This is known as a convection current. Heat also travels by radiation and conduction (see page 7).

The smoke from the fire contains black specks of soot. Soot is a powdery substance made of carbon. You also find carbon in pencil lead and charcoal. Wood contains carbon as well. Soot is unburned carbon.

 Did you know?

Very strong convection currents are set up when volcanoes erupt. Ash and smoke may be sent many miles into the sky. The warm currents of air can affect the weather hundreds of miles away.

A volcano erupting in Alaska

Burning autumn leaves

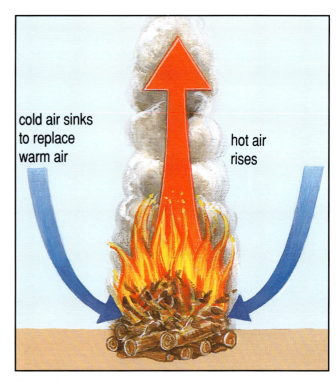

cold air sinks to replace warm air

hot air rises

Heat from the fire travels by convection.

What is a heat haze?

If you look at a burning object, such as a candle, you will see that the air above shimmers and shakes. This is a heat haze. It is caused by light, warm air rising up through colder, heavier air.

On a very hot summer's day, you may notice that the surface of the road also shimmers. This is a heat haze as well and is caused in the same way.

A heat haze above a hot road

 Did you know?

The very first fires were started by accident. They were caused by lightning hitting dry grass or a tree or by red-hot ashes from a volcano. Then about a million years ago, people learned to make fire for themselves. They struck flints or rubbed sticks together to make sparks.

Making fire by rotating a wooden stick in a hole in another piece of wood

 Did you know?

Over a million **acres** of Mediterranean forest in France, Greece, Italy, Portugal, and Spain are burned every year in forest fires. The fires have destroyed grazing land and wildlife and have added to air pollution.

Forest fires spread very quickly and can destroy large areas of land.

Why do leaves fall downward?

If you throw a ball or a stone into the air, it always comes down again. It is pulled toward the earth by the force of earth's gravity. Gravity is an invisible force that pulls different objects toward each other. But the force of the pull depends on the size of the objects. The force of gravity becomes stronger as the objects get bigger. An object needs to be as huge as the earth for its gravity to be very strong.

The earth's gravity pulls everything down toward the center of the earth. It holds the atmosphere in place around the earth (see page 27). It also holds you down onto the surface of the earth; otherwise you would float off into space. Gravity holds the moon in place in its orbit around the earth. It holds

? Did you know?

In the 17th century, the British scientist Isaac Newton was the first person to understand the force of gravity. Newton is said to have realized how gravity works after watching an apple fall from a tree.

the planets in their orbits around the sun. Gravity is also the reason why leaves fall downward from the trees.

Objects have weight because the force of gravity pulls them downward. The moon's gravity is only a sixth as strong as the earth's gravity. This means that when astronauts walk on the moon, they weigh only a sixth of their weight on earth.

The force of gravity makes leaves fall downward.

Why do plant roots grow downward?

A plant's roots anchor the plant in the ground and suck up water and minerals from the soil. The plant uses these to make its food. Roots do not grow downward by accident. The cells at the ends of a root contain starch, which collects on one side of each cell as the roots are pulled by gravity. This tells the plant which way is up and which way it should grow in order to find the things it needs. As water and minerals usually sink deep into the soil, a plant's roots therefore grow downward in order to find them.

roots growing downward

Gravity affects plants' roots.

 Did you know?

If a feather and a hammer are dropped from an airplane, gravity pulls them down at the same speed. So they should land together. Only air resistance keeps the feather from landing at the same time (see page 38).

 See for yourself

All objects have a point at which their weight balances evenly. This is called their center of gravity. Hold your palm out and try to balance a tray on it. When the tray is perfectly balanced, your palm will be under its center of gravity.

Why does rain fall faster than snow?

As an object falls through the air, the air slows it down. This is called air resistance. Some objects fall more quickly than others because they have smoother, more streamlined shapes. They do not meet as much air resistance as objects that have more irregular, spreading shapes. Raindrops have a more streamlined shape than snowflakes. This is why they fall more quickly through the air.

Sports cars and race cars have sleek, streamlined shapes to help them cut cleanly through the air. Their design reduces air resistance, or drag, so that they can go faster.

Race cars are streamlined to make them go faster.

 ## See for yourself

This simple experiment will help you see how an object's shape affects the speed at which it falls through the air. Find an 8½" x 11" piece of paper. Let the paper fall and see how long it takes to reach the ground. Now take the same piece of paper and crumple it up into a ball. Drop it from the same height as before. It will fall much more quickly because its shape is more **compact**.

You can use many different shapes and sizes of paper.

How do parachutes work?

An open parachute has a wide, spreading shape. As it floats down through the air, a lot of air pushes against it, slowing it down and helping the parachutist to land safely. Without a parachute, a person would fall quickly through the air because there would be less resistance.

⚠ See for yourself

Make your own parachute out of a square handkerchief with a thread tied to each corner. Tie the threads together and attach them to different objects, such as a matchstick or a paper clip. Then see how long it takes to parachute to the ground from a set height. Now see how long it takes for the same object to fall without the parachute.

Above: A paraglider, like a parachutist, descends slowly because of air resistance.

Right: Hang gliders glide on currents of air.

Where does space begin?

Space begins where the earth's atmosphere ends, from about 310 miles up in the sky. This does not sound far. But rockets have to travel very fast indeed, at 7 miles per second, to enter space at all. Because the earth's gravity pulls everything down toward the ground, a lot of power is needed.

Aircraft use their powerful engines to overcome air resistance. Otherwise it would slow them down (see page 38). But there is no air in space, so there is no air resistance. Once spacecraft are

(see page 38)

 Did you know?

The farthest planet from earth is Pluto. It was only discovered in 1930. The nearest star to earth, Alpha Centauri, is about 7,000 times farther away than Pluto is. Venus is the closest planet to earth. It is about 25,643,800 miles away.

moving in space, they can turn off their engines. They do not need their engines' power because there is nothing to slow them down.

Above: *The Skylab space station*

Left: *The space shuttle* Discovery *was launched in 1990. It carried a satellite into space for studying the sun.*

How big is the universe?

The universe is made up of **stars**, **planets,** and **moons**. These are grouped together in galaxies. No one knows exactly how big the universe is. The farthest that scientists can see, using a very powerful telescope, is about 6 billion light-years away (see page 42). But space probably stretches much, much farther than that. Many scientists think that the universe is still growing and getting bigger all the time.

 Did you know?

The universe contains millions of galaxies, and each galaxy has milions of stars.

This huge telescope in Australia is used for surveying the sky and studying features such as stars and galaxies.

See for yourself

To see how the universe is expanding, you will need a dark-colored balloon and a silver felt-tip marker. Draw lots of stars all over the balloon. Pretend that these are the galaxies. Now blow the balloon up and watch how the galaxies move away from each other as the universe grows bigger.

The stars grow farther away from each other as the galaxy grows bigger.

How far away are the stars?

Space itself is so incredibly huge that scientists have to use a special measurement to calculate distances within it. This measurement is called a light-year, or the distance that light travels in one year. Light travels faster than any other known thing in the universe, at 6 trillion miles in a year. So one light-year is equal to an amazing 6 trillion miles.

The nearest star to earth, after the sun, is called Alpha Centauri. It is 4.25 light-years away, or 25 trillion miles. This means that the light you see coming from this star started its journey more than four years ago.

If you could fly to Alpha Centauri in an ordinary aircraft, your journey would take more than 5 million years.

❓ Did you know?

Stars do not last forever. They are born inside clouds of dust and gas, called nebulae (1). Stars live for millions of years (2), but eventually they swell up into red giants (3). Then they shrink and become white dwarves (4). Finally they die.

Above: From this diagram of the Big Dipper, can you find the Big Dipper in the photograph on the left?

Left: Ursa Major, with the large stars of the Big Dipper

How many stars are there in space?

There are millions and millions of stars in space. But no one has ever counted them all. Our group of stars, or galaxy, is called the Milky Way. It contains about 20 trillion stars, including our sun. It is about 100,000 light-years across. But the Milky Way is just one of about 100 trillion galaxies in the universe. If each of these contained as many stars as the Milky Way, it would mean that the universe could hold 2 quintillion (2,000,000,000,000,000,000) stars!

 See for yourself

The Andromeda Galaxy is the farthest object in space that you can see without using a telescope. It contains about 40 trillion stars. It is about 2.25 million light-years away. Can you work out how far that is in miles?

The Andromeda Galaxy

Why do stars shine at night?

Stars are gigantic glowing balls made up mainly of hydrogen. In the middle of the star, the gas is constantly changing into heat and light. This is how stars make their own light, and it is why they shine.

Stars shine all the time, not just at night. They are so far away, though, that their light is very dim. During the day, the stars' light is swamped by the light coming from the sun, which is much closer to earth. You can see the stars at night because there is no sunlight. The stars seem to twinkle because their light is scattered by the atmosphere. You can learn more about the atmosphere on page 26.

 Did you know?

The brightest star in the sky is called Sirius, the Dog Star. It shines about 26 times brighter than the sun.

 Did you know?

The planet Venus seems to shine as brightly as a star. Look for it after sunset or before sunrise.

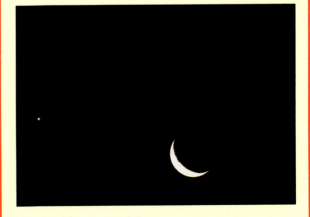

Planet Venus and the moon

Why does the moon seem to change shape?

The moon is the earth's closest neighbor in space, at a distance of 238,000 miles. It orbits the earth once every 27.3 days. During this time, it appears to change shape from a thin, crescent shape to a full circle and then back to a crescent again. The moon really stays the same shape all the time. But different amounts of it are lit by the sun, so you see different shapes. Each shape shows a **phase** of the moon.

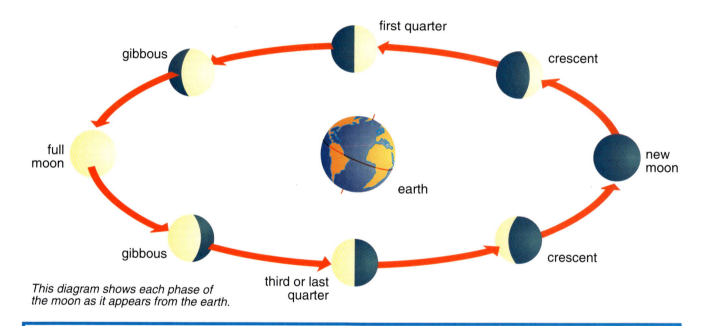

This diagram shows each phase of the moon as it appears from the earth.

first quarter

gibbous

crescent

full moon

earth

new moon

gibbous

third or last quarter

crescent

 ## See for yourself

For this experiment, you will need the fruit and stick model from page 15 and a flashlight. The model is now the moon, the light is the sun, and the person holding the moon is the earth. Ask a friend to hold the flashlight and shine it at you. Now stand in the beam and hold the moon straight up in front of you. Turn around in a circle, facing the same side of the moon all the time. Can you see how the moon waxes (grows bigger) and wanes (grows smaller) as it passes through its phases?

Which phase of the moon is showing here?

What is the dark side of the moon?

The moon takes 27.3 days to circle the earth. It also takes 27.3 days to spin once on its axis. This means that the sun only lights up one side of the moon so that, from earth, we always see the same side of the moon. We can never see the far side, or dark side, of the moon from any part of the earth.

In October 1959, the Russian space probe Luna 3 flew behind the moon and took photographs of the dark side. This was the first time that the dark side of the moon had ever been seen.

What are the dark patches on the moon?

On a clear night, you can easily see the dark patches on the moon's surface. They make a pattern that sometimes looks like a face. This is what started the story of the Man in the Moon. The dark patches are seas. But they are not full of seawater. They are great plains of **lava,** which flowed from inside the moon millions of years ago. When the lava flowed out, it was red-hot liquid rock. As it reached the surface, it cooled and became solid. The seas on the moon have wonderful names, such as the Sea of Serenity, the Ocean of Storms, and Bay of Rainbows.

The surface of the moon is also pitted with craters. These formed when meteorites (space rocks) crashed into the moon.

A crater on the dark side of the moon

Glossary

absorbed soaked up; taken in

acre one acre measures 4,840 square yards

atmosphere the layer of gases that surround the earth

bonds the connections between things that make substances stick together

compact tightly packed together

emits sends out

equator an imaginary line that passes around the earth at its fattest point, dividing the earth into two halves

expands takes up more space

galaxies systems of stars

lava hot, liquid rock that flows out of volcanoes

molecules tiny pieces of matter with which all substances are made

moons bodies that revolve around a planet

northern hemisphere the northern half of the earth above the equator

phase a certain stage that is reached

planets bodies in space that revolve around the sun and reflect the sun's light

potting compost a rich soil, full of the goodness that plants need for healthy growth

reactions changes that are sparked off by something

reflected bounced back

saturated completely soaked

southern hemisphere the southern half of the earth below the equator

stars bodies in space that do not revolve around the sun and that make their own heat and light

Further Reading

Ardley, Neil. **Heat**. New York: New Discovery Books, 1992.

Branley, Franklyn. **It's Raining Cats and Dogs: All Kinds of Weather and Why We Have It**. Boston: Houghton Mifflin, 1987.

Catherall, Ed. **Exploring Weather**. Austin, Texas: Steck-Vaughan, 1990

Dudley, Mark. **An Eye to the Sky (Adventures in Space)**. New York: Crestwood House, 1991.

Harris, Jack. **The Greenhouse Effect**. New York: Crestwood House, 1991.

Lye, Keith. **The Earth**. Brookfield, Conn: Millbrook Press, 1991.

Sauvain, Philip. **Air**. New York: New Discovery Books, 1992.

Twist, Clint. **Seas and Oceans**. New York: Dillon Press, 1992.

Index

Air, 26-29, 34-35
Air pollution, 9, 10, 27
Air pressure, 28-29
Air resistance, 37-40
Atmosphere, 7, 9, 23, 26-28,
    36, 40

Boiling, 25

Clouds, 20-22, 24, 32
    Cumulonimbus, 21
    Cumulus, 21
    Stratus, 21
Condensation, 19-20, 22
Conduction, 7, 34
Convection, 7, 34
    Currents, 34
Coriolis effect, 29

Day, 14-15

Earth's axis, 14-16
Earth's spin, 14-15
Eclipse, lunar, 13
Electricity, 10-11, 32-33
    Static, 33
Energy, 10
Evaporation, 18-20, 22

Fire, 34-35
Freezing, 24-25

Galaxies, 6, 41, 43
Gravity, 27, 36-37, 41
Greenhouse effect, 9
Greenhouses, 8

Hail, 24
Heat, 7, 34
    Ways of traveling, 7, 34
Heat haze, 35

Ice, 24-25

Leap year, 17
Light, 7, 12, 23
Lightning, 32-33
Light-years, 41, 42

Matter, states of, 25
Midnight sun, 15
Milky Way, 6, 43
Molecules, 18, 19, 23, 25
Moon, 23, 44-45
    Craters, 45
    Dark side of, 45
    Phases of, 44
    Seas, 45

Night, 14, 15

Ozone layer, 27

Plants, 8, 37

Radiation, 7, 34
Rain, 22-23, 38
Rainbows, 23

Seasons, 16-17
Shadows, 12-13
    Penumbra, 12
    Umbra, 12
Sky, color of, 23
Sleet, 22
Snow, 22, 24, 38
Snowflakes, 24
Space, 7, 23, 27, 36,
    40-43
Stars, 40-43
Sun, 6-7, 10-11, 14-15,
    27, 44
    Distance from earth, 6
    Heat and light, 7, 23
    Solar power, 10-11
    Temperature, 6
Sundial, 13
Sunrise, 23
Sunset, 23

Thunder, 32-33
Thunderstorms, 32-33

Water, 23, 24-25
Water cycle, 22
Wind, 29-31
    Direction, 29-30
    Power, 31
    Speed, 30
Windchill, 30
Wind farm, 31

Years, 17